To Jessica, for always believing in me.

WHEN GOD MADE LIGHT

Hardcover ISBN 978-1-60142-920-9
eBook ISBN 978-1-60142-921-6

Text copyright © 2018 by Matthew Paul Turner
Illustrations copyright © 2018 by David J. Catrow

Cover design by Mark D. Ford
Cover illustration by David J. Catrow

Published in the United States by WaterBrook, an imprint of the Crown Publishing Group, a division of Penguin Random House LLC, New York.

WATERBROOK® and its deer colophon are registered trademarks of Penguin Random House LLC.

The Cataloging-in-Publication Data is on file with the Library of Congress.

Printed in the United States of America
2018

10 9 8 7 6 5 4 3 2

SPECIAL SALES
Most WaterBrook books are available at special quantity discounts when purchased in bulk by corporations, organizations, and special-interest groups. Custom imprinting or excerpting can also be done to fit special needs. For information, please e-mail specialmarketscms@penguinrandomhouse.com or call 1-800-603-7051.

When God Made Light

Matthew Paul Turner   illustrated by David Catrow

WATERBROOK

Let

there

be

Light!

That's what God said.
And light began shining
and then started to spread.

It flickered and dashed.
It blinked and it flashed.
Light poured and light spilled.
It bolted and splashed.

Light glared and glimmered, it flared and sparked,

and wherever light shined, dark stopped being dark.

In the beginning
space became bright,
'cause God filled it with twinkles of yellowy white.

Brilliant stars gleamed.
Swirls of light streamed.
In that once empty space, a galaxy beamed.

When God made light,
a universe lit up,
a dazzling display of big shiny stuff.
And all that light—
every bright golden hue—
is the very same light that God put inside you.

Now, God made the sun
to light up our days,
to cover our planet with
life-filled rays.

To make summers warm
and winters not too cold,
to help flowers bloom and turn wheat
fields to gold.
To burst in the morning
at the first crack of dawn,
to rise up slowly and beam across lawns.

And when the sun shines, here's what you should do:
Go run and have fun, play a game, maybe two.
Go skipping or flipping or down a slide slipping.
Or if it's too hot, in a pool just go dipping.

Dance in the grass.
Go climbing in trees.
Build castles with sand.
Face the wind; feel its breeze.

Eat berries and cherries.
In a patch, pick strawberries.
Or whistle out loud with a choir of canaries.

And once in a while,
when the playing is done,
look up in the sky and thank God for the sun.
And when the light fades
and a day ends too soon,
wave goodbye to the sun and hello to the moon.

Yes, God made the moon
to brighten the sky's night,

to reflect the sun's shine,
to be our world's nightlight.

But beneath a dark sky, there are things you can do.
Just bring Mommy or Daddy and a flashlight or two.
Raise a tent and go camping or through the woods stamping,
romping and stomping on paths made for tramping.

Catch fireflies in jars; go gazing at stars.
Try counting and seeing how many there are.
See constellations, shapes and formations.
Find a lion or bear amid heaven's creations.

Sing songs round campfires.
Make marshmallow s'mores.
Let Grandpa tell stories.
Wage flashlight wars.

Now, when God made light,
God made all different kinds.
Some sparkles, some flares, but all light shines.
It flashes in bolts when lightning is crashing
or bursts through the sky when a comet is dashing.

And if you ever feel scared
in the darkness of night,
remember the shadows are no match for God's light.
Climb into bed,
sleep soundly and dream,
and know that inside you God's glow is agleam.

'Cause you're just like the sun and moon in the sky,
as lustrous as twinkles that dazzle the eye.

You're as splendid as lightning when it flashes so bright,
'cause on the day you were born, God said, "Let there be light!"

So beam like the sun;
    glimmer like a star.
And wherever you go,
dark will stop being dark.

Shimmer and shine,
be a beacon so bright,
'cause when God made you, child, God made light.

Matthew Paul Turner is the author of seventeen books, including the bestseller *When God Made You*. He and his wife, Jessica, live in Nashville, Tennessee, with their three children.

David Catrow is an editorial cartoonist whose vibrant illustrations have appeared in more than seventy children's books, including several *New York Times* bestsellers. He lives in Ohio with his wife, Deborah.